PENGUIN MODERN CLASSICS
The Ghosts of Meenambakkam

ASHOKAMITRAN, born in 1931 in Secunderabad, is one of the most distinguished contemporary Indian writers. In a prolific career that began in 1955, he has written over 250 short stories along with two dozen novels and novellas, in addition to a steady output of columns, essays and book reviews, earning him a central place in post-Independence Tamil literature. His work has been translated into many Indian and European languages. Five major novels as well as four collections of short fiction from his oeuvre are available in English translation. His years of rich and diverse contribution to Tamil literature have brought him many honours, including the Sahitya Akademi Award (1996). Ashokamitran lives and works in Chennai.

N. KALYAN RAMAN has published seven books of Tamil fiction in translation, including four of Ashokamitran's. His translation of contemporary Tamil poems has been published in several notable anthologies. He lives and works in Chennai.

BY THE SAME AUTHOR

Fourteen Years with Boss
Still Bleeding from the Wound
Manasarovar

ASHOKAMITRAN

The Ghosts of Meenambakkam

Translated from the Tamil by
N. Kalyan Raman

PENGUIN BOOKS
An imprint of Penguin Random House

PENGUIN BOOKS

USA | Canada | UK | Ireland | Australia
New Zealand | India | South Africa | China | Singapore

Penguin Books is part of the Penguin Random House group of companies
whose addresses can be found at global.penguinrandomhouse.com

Published by Penguin Random House India Pvt. Ltd
4th Floor, Capital Tower 1, MG Road,
Gurugram 122 002, Haryana, India

Penguin
Random House
India

First published in Tamil as *Paavam Dalpathado* in *Iruvar* by Narmada
Pathippagam, Chennai, 1988
First published in English by Penguin Books India 2016

Copyright © Ashokamitran 2016
English translation copyright © N. Kalyan Raman 2016

ISBN 9780143423270

Typeset in Dante MT Std by Manipal Digital Systems, Manipal
Printed at Manipal Technologies Limited, India

www.penguin.co.in

MIX
Paper | Supporting
responsible forestry
FSC® C043100

Translator's Note

Ashokamitran, unarguably, ranks among the great writers who have emerged in post-Independence India. Now eighty-four, he has tirelessly pursued his craft for over sixty years, contributing a prolific output of narrative fiction as well as essays and commentary on a wide range of topics. He writes nearly always in Tamil, a language he shares with 70 million native speakers in Tamil Nadu and around the world.

Although Tamil boasts of an unbroken literary tradition of over two millennia, modern literature, narrative prose fiction in particular, didn't make its advent till 1879, less than 150 years ago. In fact, truly 'modernist' writing in Tamil, giving the individual—any individual— an unprecedented centrality and agency, only began in the first half of the twentieth century. Subramania Bharathi, great poet and freedom fighter, was the pioneer of this tradition, creating a new vision of Tamil modernity. In his own way, Ashokamitran, who began writing in the 1950s, has sustained and extended this vision through his fiction, exploring human reality in an impressive range of contexts, framed inexorably by the confusions and conflicts of a reluctantly modernizing, traditional society.

Ashokamitran may have been led to this mode of exploration by the trajectory of his personal life. He is from an entirely urban background, an uncommon circumstance among Tamil writers of his generation. The son of a railway official in Secunderabad, he moved to Chennai (then Madras) in 1952, at the age of twenty-one. Soon thereafter, he found employment in the story department of Gemini Studios, a major film-production company of the time, where he worked for fourteen years. In 1966, he quit his job to become a full-time writer, a difficult but courageous decision for a person of his background and means. His work since then has earned him a pre-eminent place in the world of contemporary Tamil letters, as well as widespread national and international attention.

Any reader of Ashokamitran's fiction will immediately discern that the writer's main focus is on exploring the human predicament. His art prioritizes the experiential reality of individuals over the abstractions of history, culture, family and work, which suggests that he is moved less by ideology or intellect than by an imagination that is more forceful and illuminating than either.

Ashokamitran's narrative technique can be termed as a kind of 'documentary realism'. He describes the surface of events, apparently choosing the details with great care, but never spelling out what they might mean. In this quiet and unobtrusive way, he brings startling epiphanies and dazzling insights about the human world to the reader. It has also been observed that Ashokamitran's characters tend to be 'ordinary' people of humble circumstance, and through his nuanced account of their struggle—not always successful—to survive with dignity in hostile environments, the reader learns, more clearly than ever before, what it means to be human in these times, in this world.

Ashokamitran employs a simple language and spare prose style to suit his narrative technique. The reality he portrays is vivid and accessible, even when he is describing the inner monologue of an anguished person. His tone is normally wry and detached, punctuated not infrequently by his talent for highlighting the absurdity and humour inherent in commonplace situations.

Through his long career as a storyteller, Ashokamitran has excelled in all three formats of prose fiction: the short story, the novella and the novel. In addition to 250 short stories and ten novels, he has published over a dozen novellas— including *Paavam Dalpathado* (the Tamil original of *The Ghosts of Meenambakkam*)—which have achieved iconic status among Tamil readers. He seems to choose the novella format when he has to follow one or more characters through a brief life-journey, or which is almost the same thing, a crisis. Unlike in the short stories, the narrative in his novellas leads most often to a clear denouement. However, each novella is not so much a story as an extended meditation on the crisis. *The Ghosts of Meenambakkam* could well be a meditation on the fragility of what we think of as love in an age marked by abstract passions and random destruction.

Given the spare prose style employed by him, some believe that Ashokamitran's stories are more easily 'translatable' than the work of those whose language is more complex and descriptive. As someone who has considerable experience in translating the writer, I don't find this to be true. Ashokamitran uses details and ordinary language to convey complex realities, and unless one translates with a sure sense of what he has left unsaid, it is difficult to succeed in producing a narrative that can equal the original in literary impact. In that sense, it is certainly a challenge for the translator to navigate the intricate pathways of Ashokamitran's unique craft.

I would like to thank my editors at Penguin Books India: Tarini Uppal, for her support and gentle guidance through the making of this book, and Arpita Basu, for her contribution towards improving the quality of the translation. Any errors that remain are of course mine.

Chennai   N. Kalyan Raman
February 2016

1

Road accidents have been happening since the time roads came into existence. Manuneedhi Chozhan's[1] reputation as a just king hinges on a road accident. Karnan's desperate plight during the Kurukshetra war, with his chariot wheels stuck in the mud, is the result of a road accident he was involved in much earlier. A major tangle that develops at the end of Charles Dickens's *A Tale of Two Cities* is caused by a road accident in one of the initial chapters. Madame Defarge, the lady with a heart of steel who precipitates the final tragedy, is introduced during this road accident.

The statistics on road accidents in Madras were presented to the public on a billboard in the Thousand Lights junction of Anna Salai. Several accidents took place, we were told, when people tried to read the figures on this giant billboard.

Accidents didn't happen on all roads. On China Bazaar Road, through which lakhs of vehicles and pedestrians passed daily, accidents were rare. On Egmore's Kennet Lane, used daily by thousands of travellers and hundreds of buses, there were hardly any accidents. But on GST—Grand Southern Trunk—Road, in front of Meenambakkam airport, there was an accident nearly every day. Why did the city corporation, which had installed bright lights in many other areas, keep this place dark? If it was true that everyone who died of unnatural causes hovered eternally over the site of their death, then thousands of ghosts must have been loitering in front of the airport. Was that why lives were being lost there again and again?

The first time I went to the airport, the world was in perfect order. I had to visit the Madras Flying Club, the address of which was given as just 'Meenambakkam airport'. In those days, the airport remained deserted for several hours during the day, with no sign of human presence. Anyone could walk in and take a tour of the premises. There was a white line painted on the floor, along with the words: Do not cross this line. However, I knew that we could go right up to a plane to receive a passenger. It was possible to have them open the door, move the stairway to the plane, put a famous movie star on board and send him off even after the engine had started. But on this first visit to the airport, I couldn't find anyone to tell me the way to the Flying Club. Over time, the airport became livelier. A couple of policemen arrived first; then, an entry ticket costing one rupee, which was raised to two rupees after a few days; later, heavy police presence and anti-hijacking measures. Meanwhile, the airport grew even bigger. Initially I had to go once a year; at the most, twice. Since my visits to the airport occurred after long intervals, even small changes were clearly visible to me.

After a certain stage, I had to go to the airport almost daily. The studio I worked for had started making Hindi films. For these films, we flew down all our lead actors from Bombay. This was five or six years ago. After that, I didn't go anywhere near the airport for several years. One day a plane heading from Bombay to Madras caught fire immediately after taking off and crashed. By the evening of the next day, long black caskets, with charred bodies inside, had landed in Madras. My daughter's was one among those bodies. Naturally, I was expected to go to the airport and receive the body. But I was nauseous all day, starting early that morning. By evening, my nausea had become unbearable. Anyway, I wouldn't have accomplished anything special by going there. The caskets were nailed shut. They had somehow identified the bodies in Bombay itself and marked the caskets accordingly. Some people advised us not to open them. A man who opened a casket became unhinged right there, we were told. The casket with my daughter's name on it wasn't even brought home. They took it directly to the cremation ground in Kannammapettai. I couldn't even attend the cremation.

As I stood now in the veranda outside the airport around nine at night, the people who had gathered there looked like evil spirits to me. I wondered whether this was the result of reading frequent reports about murders that our media dished out with increasing proficiency. The airport seemed like a better place to reflect on death than a cremation ground.

The entry fee was further raised from two to four rupees, and later they completely banned everyone except passengers. And since entry was banned, there was no entry fee either.

Like me, hundreds of people were standing in that narrow outer veranda, anticipating a variety of hardships. There was no place for anyone to sit. So our legs inevitably began to hurt. Many people in that crowd might have brought their cars, but if it started raining before the plane arrived, they couldn't avoid getting drenched. Those who had arranged to come by bus or taxi because they did not own cars, carried umbrellas. Madras had only one airport in those days. From the airport you had to walk nearly a mile to reach Meenambakkam railway station. If it was daytime and you didn't have a lot of luggage, you could catch a bus. The thirty-odd taxis parked in front of the airport looked like crouching tigers ready to pounce. There was a bus called 'Pallavan coach'. Its stops were convenient for foreign travellers, but not necessarily for the locals. This coach was never of any use to me. And I had yet to meet a taxi driver who did not harass me. It was nearing ten. The sky was dark with impending rain. It was the kind of situation that could tempt even a virtuous taxi driver.

After ten I fell asleep on my feet for twenty minutes. Suddenly there was a crescendo of ear-splitting noise: a plane had just landed. It was parked close to the terminal building for the convenience of the passengers. There was a mild stir of excitement inside and outside the airport. I pressed my face against the glass wall of the terminal building to check which flight had landed. It was a flight from Singapore. Scheduled to land at three or three-thirty in the afternoon, it had arrived at half past ten. The crowd standing outside must have been waiting for this flight.

For all the passengers from Singapore, it was going to be a sleepless night. They were crammed, along with their hand luggage, into a gigantic glass enclosure. Just when everyone was exhausted from waiting and ready to drop, the customs inspection began. In all of human history, you wouldn't find anything like the mutual suspicion and distrust that prevailed there right then. Every passenger was carrying a portable radio-cum-cassette player, as if it were their ticket for the journey. Since the inspection was unavoidable because of the gadget in their hands, they would have to wait inside the glass cage with palpitating hearts. Totally unconcerned about the ordeal they were going through, their relatives outside the airport could think of nothing but the foreign items in the travellers' baggage. This made their long wait for the customs inspection even grimmer.

I, too, looked around as much as I could. The passengers from Singapore were dressed in flashy clothes. Uncharacteristically, even the westerners among them wore outfits that were a bit loud.

Leaving the passengers from Singapore to their worries, I stood watching the trucks and buses pass on the road in front of the airport. My left leg hurt more than the right. If this continued, and, after a few minutes, if someone came to chop my leg off, I would probably stand still, raising no objection. I might have even begged him to amputate my left leg.

Many among those who had come to receive the Singapore passengers had brought their families, including young children. Forgetting all about their excitement over gifts like Singapore dolls, chocolate, face powder, soap and the two-in-one, these children had curled up to sleep in every available nook and corner of that veranda. A visit to the airport did not happen often in their lives. In those days, the only mode of travel to and from Singapore was by air. That was the main reason for their visit to the airport.

I found a spot along the wall and sat down. Right beside me sat a family: husband, wife and three children. The husband could have come to the airport alone, leaving his wife and children at home. But they must have insisted on coming; or they might have travelled to Madras from a small town to receive this passenger tonight. They must have been waiting after having arrived straight from the railway station to the airport. This practice of the entire family coming to the airport and waiting there was more common in the case of passengers arriving from Arab countries. Singapore was a leisure destination. The socio-economic status of travellers to and from Singapore was very different from that of passengers from Arab countries. Those arriving from Arab countries might bring in a lot of money and goods, but they were by no means affluent.

The head of the family asked me, 'Sir, where can I buy milk here at this time?'

'The food stalls on the main road must have shut by now. You can buy milk from the tea shop, though.'

I thought he would set out immediately to buy milk, but he continued to sit there. I felt like closing my eyes for a few minutes. Then he asked me, 'Have your people arrived?'

'What?'

'Have your people arrived by this flight? Have you met them already?'

'No. What about yours?'

'My grand-uncle has arrived. He is sitting in front of that pillar over there.'

I looked in the direction in which he was pointing. There were dozens of passengers sitting there. A few were standing. Nearly everyone was smoking. I spotted someone I hadn't noticed till then. I remembered having seen him—sometime, somewhere. I couldn't recall his name. But that face had not vanished from my memory. Where had I seen him? Who was he?

But I couldn't worry about him for too long. The plane from Bombay was about to land.

The arrival of the Bombay flight caused even more excitement than the one from Singapore, both within the airport and in the veranda outside. All the passengers on the Bombay flight had to disembark in Madras. So their number would be at least double that of passengers from the Singapore flight. Second, these passengers could pick up their bags and go home immediately. There would be no delay on account of immigration formalities, customs inspection and conversion of foreign currency.

After the plane finally came to a halt, passengers started disembarking. They would enter another mammoth glass enclosure. Their bags and suitcases would be transported from the plane and placed on a horizontally laid, carousel-like contraption in another hall. As the bags went round and round on the carousel, the passengers had to pull them off the belt. Then they could simply walk out.

I moved closer to the exit door for passengers. Like devotees at a temple waiting for a glimpse of sacred light, dozens of people were already waiting there. Their eyes were no longer drowsy. They stood impossibly alert, staring intently at the door. Many among them were drivers, that is, those who drove for their masters. The master himself was unable to come to the airport at that unearthly hour to receive his guest. Some drivers did not know the identity of the guest they had come to receive. So they had written down the guest's name in big, block letters on a placard or large sheet, and held it up in front of the exit door. Those who spent thousands of rupees travelling by plane must be men of wealth and influence. Those who received them must also be men of great wealth and influence; or they must have come to the airport on behalf of such wealthy men. But even such people were forced to demean themselves in this manner, pushing and jostling with others on a narrow veranda in front of a small door.

Twisting and contorting my body, I had somehow forced my way to the front of a queue. One by one, the passengers began to come out. Passengers with heavy luggage walked out pushing trolleys on which their bags were stacked. Black, dusky foreigners; men, women, children; and suddenly, a familiar face. The face of someone I had seen only a short while ago among a group of Singapore passengers. How had he joined this group of domestic passengers? Anyone who knew even a little about airport procedures would insist that this was impossible. But this man had slipped very easily out of the inspection enclosure and mingled with a group that was not subjected to any checks. He was someone I knew, someone I had met, talked to and spent time with. But who, where and when, I couldn't recall immediately.

Even the Bombay passengers had to prove that the luggage they were carrying was actually theirs before they could approach the exit gate. But this man had only a shoulder bag and, therefore, he was not stopped.

Near the exit door, a fat foreign woman was staggering forward with her heavy suitcases. He was walking right behind her. That lady walked through the exit door and past me. He followed. He was less than a foot away from me.

'Dalpathado!' I shouted involuntarily. I had recalled his name.

For one-thousandth of a second, he paused in his stride. Then, as if my calling out had nothing to do with him, he walked on.

Both his attention and mine must have been focused on the other person; it was indeed so. At the same time, we were alerted by a strange sensation. As soon as I had said 'Dalpathado', I had sensed that two people in that crowd had stopped suddenly, their eyes wide with surprise and bodies rigid. But after Dalpathado moved away even farther, this detail faded from my attention. I should have watched them both closely and remembered their faces.

But Dalpathado had seen them, I came to know later.

2

Within fifteen minutes, the hall where the Bombay passengers had gathered became deserted. Even the airport staff had disappeared from there. A security guard could still have been hiding somewhere, keeping the area under surveillance.

Somehow, when you were in the vicinity of Meenambakkam airport late at night, your thoughts turned unavoidably perverse.

My work was over. This must be my fate too, or else, why would I keep visiting the airport again and again? Once the customs inspection for the Singapore passengers got under way and they started coming out, the main road would get busy. Before that happened, I had to reach Meenambakkam railway station.

I walked slowly along GST Road and reached the shortcut that led to Meenambakkam railway station. Even in the dark, I could see GST Road running straight for nearly a mile before turning. From where I was standing, I could see the construction site for another airport terminal. Although I couldn't really see the work that was being carried out briskly under a host of bright lights, I could certainly hear it. The distant rumble of giant machines mixing cement, blue metal stone and sand together, and pouring out concrete accentuated the silence of the night. Instead of going to the railway station, I walked further along the road. My head was filled with thoughts of the new terminal building. From this terminal, situated around a mile and a half away from the present one, planes would depart and arrive; passengers would depart and arrive. Some would arrive laughing; some, worried; and a few others as charred corpses . . .

There was open space on either side of the road—rail tracks to the left and the airport's long runway to the right. The runway alone was common to both terminals. This too was a bit like the railways. The rail track was common, and along the track, a series of railway stations.

The hillocks of Pallavaram appeared like silhouettes in the distance. The dark clouds in the sky seemed to be pressing down on the earth's atmosphere and choking it. Without understanding exactly why, I was walking down that road in the darkness and rain.

There was a flash of lightning. I saw Dalpathado on the road a hundred yards ahead of me. Though we were both walking, I walked with an air of freedom. Dalpathado seemed to crouch as he walked, as though he was on the run. He was also carrying in his hand something that looked like a suitcase. I had seen him with only a shoulder bag when he had come out of the airport. Where had the suitcase come from?

I quickened my pace. When I recognized him back at the airport, he pretended not to care and then disappeared. But surely he couldn't do that now, when he found himself all alone on open ground.

Since I had glimpsed his silhouette in the momentary flash of lightning, I could see him clearly in the dark. The same gait—without a doubt, it was Dalpathado.

A car passed me from behind at great speed. Its red tail lights raced away in the dark like sparks from a blaze. Suddenly it swerved dangerously to the left. Dalpathado was walking in that very spot. It wasn't clear whether the car had swerved towards him first or he had jumped away of his own volition. As soon as the beam of the headlight fell on him, he leapt, suitcase in hand. The car turned back on to the road and sped away.

I ran forward. The collision must have dismembered Dalpathado and scattered his limbs.

When I reached the spot where the car might have hit him, the vehicle which had sped away was coming back towards me from the opposite direction. In one swift leap, I hid myself in the hollow next to the road. The car passed that spot seconds later. After travelling a short distance, it turned back.

Rolling on the ground, I moved away from the road. The car stopped. Two men got out and searched for Dalpathado along the roadside with the help of a flashlight.

I was lying flat on the ground. I could hear them talk, but couldn't catch what they were saying.

During those five or six minutes, there was hardly any traffic on GST Road. Then vehicles started to appear again. Three buses went south, one after another. A jeep-like vehicle drove by and halted near the car driven by those two men. It must have been a police vehicle. The voices I heard were typical of policemen. The policemen questioned both men. It was all over in two minutes! The car drove away. The police vehicle, too, left immediately, in the opposite direction.

It took me a while to muster the courage to stand up. The blades of grass on the hard ground felt like thorns. Apart from that, there were real thorn bushes and lots of insects. Before long I encountered snakes and scorpions. I stood up and walked towards the road slowly. I was certain that Dalpathado must still be lying there somewhere.

Suddenly, I had an idea that dismayed me. Why hadn't I raised an alarm when the policemen had stopped there? Surely, those two people in the car were going up and down the road only with the intention of doing away with Dalpathado. Would I ever get a better opportunity to hand them over to the police and protect Dalpathado? I had committed a blunder.

Overcome with contrition, I started searching for him and called out, 'Dalpathado! Dalpathado!' But was he in a condition to hear my voice? If a Fiat car travelling at sixty miles an hour had crashed into a man, just surviving the collision would have been a miracle.

There was a large hollow in the ground a little away from the road. Thrown by the collision, Dalpathado could have fallen into it. I walked towards it. In the darkness, I could only see a pool of stagnant water at the bottom. 'Dalpathado! Dalpathado!' I called out.

'Shh! Shh!' I heard a sound that seemed to come from the vicinity of the hollow.

'Dalpathado!'

Suddenly I felt someone's hand gripping mine, trying to pull me down. I shouted 'Dalpathado!' again.

'Don't shout, you fool! Now you're going to get killed along with me,' he said.

My panic and feeling of contrition had abated and I lay flat on the ground. I was not wrong: He was indeed Dalpathado. During one of the international film festivals held in India a long time ago, he was one of the foreign film-makers in attendance. His film *Paranimaaru* had received the Best Film award at the festival. When he and other eminent people from the film fraternity stayed in Madras for a week, I, along with a colleague, had escorted those twenty delegates and then sent them off to their home towns.

Dalpathado glanced up briefly from the hollow. 'Shh! Crawl along the road and reach the rail tracks. Make sure that light from the trains doesn't fall on you. At the right moment, cross the tracks and slip into the playground on the other side,' he said.

I've been told that I started walking only when I turned two. So my experience in crawling must be considerable. Even so, crawling on the hard ground next to the tracks between Pallavaram and Meenambakkam stations in the dead of night was not easy for me. I had to reach home before dawn and change my clothes. Otherwise, I would have to keep explaining myself to everyone I met.

Since I had feared that I would only see him as a battered corpse, I was surprised and pleased by Dalpathado's energy. Dragging his suitcase, he was moving rapidly in the direction of the tracks. An electric train passed south. It was midnight. A train would arrive from the opposite direction in half an hour. If I had to reach home and get at least an hour of sleep, that train was my last chance.

It seemed beyond my grasp. Why did I go to the airport? What was I doing there? How was this man related to me? Just because he told me to roll on the ground, I was doing it. Why was I passing my time in such a foolish manner?

I stood up. A few yards ahead, Dalpathado hissed at me, gravely upset: 'Lie down! Lie down! Don't raise your head!'

The force of urgency in his voice left me with no option but to duck down. However, somewhat aggrieved, I hissed back, 'Why do I have to crawl with you like a snake?'

'Your destiny changed the moment you recognized me,' said Dalpathado. 'No use talking about it any more. I will keep you safe tonight. Later, we'll see.'

I lay completely still.

'Please do as I say at least for the next thirty minutes. Those two are going to come back. We must get away without being seen by them.'

'Who are they? Why should I get away?'

'Please, let us cross the tracks now. Then I'll tell you everything.'

'Who are those two men?'

'All right, I'll tell you this much. They were also waiting at the airport. As soon as you called out my name, I knew that your life was in danger too.'

The 12.30 a.m. train sped past in the direction of Beach station. After it passed us, Dalpathado and I crossed the tracks. What had been a slight drizzle had turned into a downpour. Dalpathado ran ahead in the dark of the night with his head down. I trailed him like a shadow. I could catch a train only after four in the morning. After a sleepless night, it would be impossible to keep awake the next morning. All normal functions of the body would have been impaired. Yet, in spite of my fifty years, I was running behind a foreigner in the pouring rain in the middle of the night—it would make no sense at all to anyone!

Even though it was dark, Dalpathado raced ahead without running into any obstacles as though it was familiar terrain for him. The ground was not only rough, every now and then we came across rocks too. To one side was a big hillock. Looking still more intently, I saw several hillocks in a row.

After we circled past the first hillock, four or five houses were dimly visible in the distance. This place must be a lake, I thought. If the rain continued to beat down, those houses could only be accessed by boat.

Dalpathado seemed to be familiar with the trails in the area even in the dark. That he walked so fast while carrying a suitcase, with neither doubt nor hesitation, amazed me.

'Dalpathado,' I called out.

He stopped.

'I'll stop here. Let me go on home,' I told him in English.

'I am very sorry. You can't leave.'

'Why not?'

'We could be in danger at this very moment. Please come along with me for just half a mile. The situation may clear up tomorrow morning.'

His tone seemed to be half pleading, half threatening. In my condition, I lacked the strength to argue my case. So I followed him.

As we drew closer, the houses seemed like haystacks. All the doors and windows were tightly shut. Perhaps the residents did not want any light to shine through gaps or cracks. Or maybe they wanted to keep the raging wind and rain out. Even on normal days, the area couldn't have enjoyed any protection from the elements. In the rainy season, life must have been even more difficult. If people were living there despite all the hardship, there could only be a couple of reasons for it: the desire to live under one's own roof even if it was in the back of beyond, or the lack of means to afford a comfortable home. These were the only two reasons that occurred to me.

Dalpathado walked up to the third house. 'Sivanesan! Sivanesan!' He called out through clenched teeth. He knocked on the door twice with his index finger. His calling and knocking were not clearly audible even to me. But we heard the sound of a latch being drawn back. There wasn't a single light in the entire house; it was completely dark amidst the surrounding blackness. It was only from the sound that I guessed the door was being opened. Dalpathado entered first. Then he said, 'You also come in, sir.'

Tripping and falling down in the dark comes with a minor advantage. No one else can laugh at your clumsiness. There is no other benefit.

With much hesitation, I took a step forward and crossed something that looked like a threshold. Immediately, I heard the door being shut behind me. After it was bolted, the flick of a switch was heard.

For the first time that night, I saw Dalpathado in proper light.

Dalpathado forced a smile on his face when we were directly in front of each other. His smile seemed to convey the unbearable sadness of many long years.

The third person in the room lit a candle and placed it on the floor; then he turned off the electric light. He handed a few lungis to Dalpathado.

Both of us were standing near the door. Rainwater dripping from our bodies and clothes had collected in small puddles at our feet. The suitcase that Dalpathado had been carrying with him was missing. The third person had already hidden it somewhere.

Dalpathado removed his coat and dropped it where he was standing. Throwing a lungi at me, he said, 'Please dry your head.' He also removed his shirt and vest, and dropped them on the floor. No matter how quickly he shed them, water dripped all around.

I started removing my shirt and vest. Outside, the wind and rain were raging with a low growl. The candle flame threw our shadows on the walls and ceiling. After towelling my head with the lungi, I wrapped it around my waist.

In a room adjoining ours, there was a large mat spread on the floor. Dalpathado motioned me in that direction. I lurched into the room like an intoxicated man. My eyes, which had got used to the dark by then, led me to a section of the mat. I sat down. A moment later, I had slumped on my side.

Outside, I could still hear the relentless lashing of the wind and rain.

suitcases

3

'You must have heard, surely? Lalitha is planning to go on a tour.'

'She said goodbye to me when she left yesterday, but she never mentioned anything about a tour.'

'Didn't she? But weren't you talking about suitcases and bags yesterday?'

'Were we? I don't remember. That man from the corner house passed by, lugging a suitcase, and we made a few comments. That was all.'

'I thought you two were chatting for a long time. Until I finished making the *bajjis*,[2] all I seemed to hear was talk about bags and suitcases.'

'Well, in a way our talk was about bajjis. One day that man was carrying brinjals from the market in his briefcase, she said, and we laughed about it. She said nothing about a tour.'

'Didn't she tell you anything about her passport application?'

'Passport? No! Why would she need a passport?'

'For her tour.'

'I see.'

'Aiyo, you seem to know nothing at all! She told me that she and her husband are going on a foreign tour for twenty days. She is planning to leave the children with us while she is away. I told her to have a word with her father, just in case.'

'Is that really necessary? As it is, don't you look after the children half the time?'

'She is going on this trip because her husband wants to take her along. Do you know what her mother-in-law had to say?'

'Nobody tells me anything. I only hear it from you.'

'I believe she said, "Lalitha is still at a stage where she has to wash diapers. Why does she want a foreign tour now?"'

'Did she say this to Lalitha? But Lalitha doesn't have to wash diapers, does she? She has three or four maids to do the job.'

'Does a woman need a reason to rebuke her daughter-in-law?'

'But anyone could say what she did, right? The younger child is not even a year old.'

'Do people who work stay away from the office just because they have to wash diapers?'

'Is going to work the same as going on a foreign tour?'

This argument went on for a long time but I took no further part in it. Inwardly, I was glad that Lalitha was set to cross the seas. I hadn't done anything for Lalitha. In fact, no father could have raised a girl child and married her off with such little effort. Plain clothes, simple food and no presents, sweets or new dresses for festivals—I had brought up my child like a refugee from an orphanage. As in the film *Parasakthi*, the company I worked for had a good reputation but paid poorly. In fact, its employees could only live like the inmates of an orphanage. My wife complained over and over again about the lack of money. Lalitha never said a word about it. She used each pencil for three months. Not once did she buy new textbooks. She never asked me to buy her ice cream nor insisted on going to the cinema. Her skirts and *davani*[3] were invariably stitched out of her mother's old saris. She managed without any footwear till she was in the tenth standard. Living with dignity while accepting her poverty was her inborn trait. Such maturity was beyond her mother.

But I always wondered if this maturity, patience, tolerance and forbearance were traits and principles invented by the impotent to ennoble and thereby deceive themselves. I spent many a night staring at the ceiling, brooding over how Lalitha had been forced to deceive herself in this way since her childhood. There was no such thing as privacy in the world today. A man's prospects, helplessness, affluence, poverty, rage and jealousy were bared to the world all the time. None might be interested in knowing all this about him, but the fact that it was lying exposed was enough to shrink his heart with shame. Since it had been decided at the outset that only so much was possible in life for my wife and me, our torment was reduced considerably. My wife complained once in a while, but I had wiped my heart clean, dried it in the sun and put it away. But had it been possible for Lalitha? She had so many friends and more than a few acquaintances! However, she was equally friendly with everyone. Many of her friends were indeed from poor families, but at least a few of them must have been of a kind to exacerbate a little girl's feelings of deprivation. Lalitha didn't seem flustered in any way. As a sixteen-year-old, she never asked for a new skirt or a pair of earrings in the latest style or a new handkerchief—never asked me, at any rate. Had she perhaps, because I spent so little time at home, fulfilled all her needs through her mother?

But suddenly one day, her life took a major turn. Rajagopalan, who was by some convoluted reckoning a distant uncle of mine, came to stay in our house for a day. The next month, we received a letter from him asking for Lalitha's horoscope. When her marriage to his son was conducted in January the following year, Lalitha had not yet turned twenty-one.

All this was beyond my capacity and totally incompatible with my means. Yet, Lalitha had suddenly become a rich woman. Her husband, Ranganathan, cherished and nurtured her—like the eye beneath the lid, as it were. But if someone was lucky enough to have got a girl with Lalitha's sweet nature as a wife, why wouldn't he cherish her? There was someone, however, who thought otherwise—Ranganathan's mother.

She had taken a strong dislike to Lalitha, perhaps because she had not played her due part in selecting her daughter-in-law; or because her son and husband were closer to Lalitha than she was; or because Lalitha had not obsequiously sought anything from her; or because she was unable to understand a human being who was truly and wholly content, regardless of what she did or did not possess.

Buoyed by the profits they had earned that year, Ranganathan's business partners decided that the four of them would go on a world tour along with their wives: twenty-eight days, fifteen countries, nineteen cities.

Lalitha was quite reluctant to accompany them leaving her children behind. Her second child was not even a year old. Neither child was of an age to withstand the rigours of such an arduous tour. They would not understand anything either. If they were taken along, they would suffer. Besides, they would not spare their parents enough free time to enjoy the tour. Ranganathan insisted that they must leave the children behind. Everyone, including him, knew that his mother would not take care of them.

All of us went to the airport to send off Lalitha and her husband. In those days, we were allowed inside the terminal building. We had to pay the entry fee, though. Inside, there was a throng of people. Along with the fifteen people in our group, there were Ranganathan's partners, as well as their families and friends, bringing the total to over sixty. Besides, there were so many other passengers and their kith and kin who had come to see them off! Lalitha must have wanted to spend a few private moments with her older child. But whenever she got near the child, somebody would idiotically congratulate her on her first trip abroad and immediately request her to bring back a Japanese sari for them. Lalitha held on to the child's hand but was unable to speak a word to him.

Lalitha's in-laws too had accompanied them to the airport. There was no problem where the father-in-law was concerned. But Lalitha's mother-in-law kept summoning her to tell her something or the other. With only half an hour left until departure, we were told that we could not continue chatting in the lounge, and Lalitha and Ranganathan went inside. Lalitha kept turning back to look at us as she walked away.

That was the last time I saw Lalitha. She came back in a black casket, as a corpse or simply ashes—I didn't even see the casket.

Ranganathan had survived. At the end of their world tour, when they returned to Bombay, their plane arrived three hours later than scheduled. The daytime flight from Bombay to Madras had already left. Just because she had travelled around the world by plane, did she also need to fly from Bombay to Madras? Couldn't she go by train, something that people like her were used to? The tour ticket was for a round trip that began and ended in Madras. Therefore, even if it was ten days before a flight became available, she would have to return by air.

For Ranganathan, a three-day stopover in Bombay promised many benefits. Missing the flight to Madras filled him inwardly with unanticipated joy. But Lalitha was on tenterhooks. Being away from her children for a whole month had not seemed all that hard, but a further delay of a few hours was simply unbearable. She had never made such a request to Ranganathan until then: Could she at least speak to the children on the telephone? Surprised, Ranganathan arranged to book a trunk call from the airport to his house in Madras. Even if the children recognized their mother's voice on the telephone, they could not understand a word she said.

Lalitha and her husband learnt that a flight was to leave for Madras at one in the morning,

and she refused to budge from the Bombay
airport. Ranganathan got her a seat on that
flight. Bearing gifts for her children and for
relatives and acquaintances, Lalitha started
at midnight for Madras. It must have been
twenty-four hours since she had last slept, so
she must have fallen asleep immediately after
boarding. At ten past one, the plane caught fire
and plummeted down. Lalitha might not have
realized that life was leaving her.

4

'Lalitha!' I woke up screaming. There must have been daylight outside, but because of the rain, which was still pouring down, it was quite dark.

Dalpathado came rushing to the room I was in, flashlight in hand. 'What? What happened?' he said in Tamil.

I couldn't reply immediately. When he asked me again, I asked him in turn, 'What time is it?'

'Six o'clock. What happened? I thought a bandicoot had come into the house,' he started speaking in English as usual.

'It was no bandicoot, but another bandicoot might have sneaked in, after all.'

Dalpathado was silent, unable to understand what I was saying. Then he said, 'Will you have a cup of tea? Mr Sivanesan is going to make tea.'

'Who is Sivanesan?'

'He is the man who opened the door for us last night.'

Not only was I confused by my memories, my body too was in a state of near collapse. I lay down on the floor again.

Water had leaked from the roof and formed a puddle in a corner of the room. The residents of this house must be very poor. Floor, roof, wall and door—everything there spoke of indigence.

Dalpathado returned after a few minutes with piping hot tea in a glass tumbler. With the very first sip, I knew that it had been prepared using milk powder.

Dalpathado also brought a glass of tea for himself and sat down beside me. 'Could it be twenty years since the last time we met?'

I gave my brain a good shake. 'Twenty-two years,' I said.

'How do you still remember me?'

'I don't know.'

'You recognized me. If you had just moved on, there would have been no trouble at all. You followed me down the road. Those people who stalked us last night will still keep coming after us.'

'How is Sylvia doing?'

Dalpathado's face grew dark. If he was forced to reply, he would feel extremely awkward. As if to grant him a small reprieve, Sivanesan entered the room with a tumbler of tea. Like Dalpathado, he sat on the floor facing me. 'I have known sir for more than twenty years,' said Dalpathado to Sivanesan.

Sivanesan's suspicious eyes did not register even a flicker. 'Is that so?' he said.

'How is Sylvia?' I asked Dalpathado again. Sivanesan raised an eyebrow. Then he went out of the room.

Dalpathado looked intently at me. Then he said, 'I don't know.'

'Why?'

'A very simple reason. It's been many years since I saw her last.'

'Really?'

'Yes.'

'Why? At that time, you were her whole world.'

'Maybe I was. But that world itself is not constant, is it? Besides, people live in many worlds at once, don't they?'

'That's true enough.'

He got up and opened the window. The sky was pale and it was raining incessantly.

I tried to stand up. The unusual exertions of the previous night made my body ache all over. It was a miracle that I had not come down with a fever after getting drenched in the rain.

'Dalpathado, I must go home now,' I said.

'It's still raining, sir. Please wait for half an hour. I'll make arrangements.'

'Are you staying here? But you were with those Singapore passengers last night!'

'You are surely mistaken.'

'My brain hasn't become that dull yet.'

'I'll have a word with Sivanesan and get back.'

I was beginning to get angry with myself. Why and for what reason was I trapped in such a place among such people?

Suddenly, a deep sense of sorrow welled up inside me. Unable to stifle my grief, I sobbed aloud. It was like the scream of an animal which found itself in mortal danger. Both Sivanesan and Dalpathado came running.

'What happened, sir?' asked Dalpathado. He came near me and held me by the shoulders.

'Easy, sir, easy,' he said.

He would never know the source of my grief or its magnitude.

5

There was another thing that Dalpathado did not know about Sylvia. Twenty-two years ago, after I had arranged a taxi for him in front of Hotel Oceanic, I waited in the reception lounge. Sylvia had to come there eventually.

She arrived at eleven. A close look revealed that she had been crying. 'Miss Morris,' I said. She noticed me then and offered a faint smile.

'May I speak to you about something?'

'What is it?'

'Can we go up to your room?'

As she briskly led the way, I clambered up behind her. We took the stairs; the lift was still not working.

The hotel staff had not cleaned her room yet.

'Professor Dubley . . .' Sylvia began.

Professor Dubley was a Frenchman. He had made a few outstanding movies even before the Second World War. His films were part of the curriculum in many film institutes around the world. It was he who had given the award to Dalpathado's film at the festival.

'I know. I've come here straight from the hospital.'

'What do they say?'

'He is in the intensive care unit. They were trying to send word to his relatives in France.'

'He doesn't have any close relatives. It has been several years since his wife passed away. He is a Catholic, I hope you know that!'

'Is he? I didn't know.'

'He told me that he had only an elder sister. She lives in an old-age home.'

'On cinema, especially on things related to film techniques, people here in India consult only Professor Dubley. He is such a renowned expert. But now when he is dying, not even a local relative can be with him.'

'If he had died in his own country, thousands would have gathered outside the hospital.'

'I came to ask you about something.'

'What is it?'

'Is Mr Dalpathado in trouble?'

'I don't understand.'

'Only Mr Sharma and I got to know the festival delegates to some extent. I am concerned about Mr Dalpathado.'

'Then you should convey your concern to him. It has nothing to do with me.'

'I see. Forgive me. I thought I'd rather talk to you instead of him before taking any decision.'

Sylvia appeared to have changed her mind. 'What are you talking about?'

'Mr Dalpathado has borrowed money from all sorts of people. He is selling all the items he has brought from his country. There is nothing wrong with foreign tourists leaving a few gifts behind but if he is selling goods which carry a customs duty in India, he can be charged with a criminal offence.'

Sylvia was silent.

'If he tells me or Mr Sharma, we will try our best to help him.'

'Do you know that he is a man of considerable wealth in his country?'

'It's not uncommon for people to run into money trouble when they are abroad.'

'Do you know anything about the articles he sold?'

'No. But a smuggler who is well known among the local policemen comes here often to meet him.'

Sylvia stared at me for a moment. 'He even tried to sell me,' she said.

I was silent, not knowing what to say.

'I left my parents, siblings and everyone else for his sake. Here, he is trying to sell me.'

Sylvia started crying suddenly. I moved closer to her. 'I know,' I said.

'So, after you found out, what are you all doing about it? Aren't you human beings?'

'I am also young. I must be the same age as you. But a man's experience is quite different. In this country, in the film industry. . .'

'I am not a movie slut.'

'You have come here with a film personality. You are staying with him. You have acted with him in films.'

'So what?'

'You'll be perceived only as a movie star. That apart, there is another thing that has made your position weak.'

'What?'

'The trouble with Professor Dubley.'

Sylvia was furious.

'That man is dying. Don't slander him.'

'That's only since this morning. It wasn't so through the whole of last week, was it?'

'No. I knew about it in Delhi. I knew it when he gave the award to Dalpathado. That was the first time I met Professor Dubley. I could sense that he wouldn't last another four days.'

'Is that right?'

'Yes. Whatever happened between me and him was with the certain knowledge that his end was quite near.'

'End?'

'Yes. I thought it would come in four days. Now it's taken fourteen days, that's all.'

'Was he aware of that?'

'I don't know. Do we really know what we think we know? Whatever it was that made me think that his end was near, he must have known it too. But it's possible that he didn't think of it as a sign of approaching death, isn't it? He did of course believe that he was going to live another ten years.'

We were silent for a while. By then, Sylvia's face had cleared up.

'You are also leaving Madras tonight, aren't you?'

'I don't know. I wonder what Dalpathado has planned. I am going to stay on in India for a few more days.'

'Here?'

'Yes . . . what were you asking—in this hotel? No. I am going to check out in half an hour.'

'This film festival has caused a rift between husband and wife.'

'Dalpathado and I are not "husband and wife", nor could we ever be. If we had not parted here today, we would have parted somewhere else. It's fortunate that I have relatives and acquaintances in this country. I was able to protect myself. If it was a festival held in a European city, he would have pushed me into bed with ten or fifteen men by now.'

'You are very hard on Mr Dalpathado.'

'I didn't know that you were so close to him.'

'To me, he was just like all the other delegates attending the festival. But among all of them, he was the one who seemed to be in some kind of pain all the time.'

I began to go down the stairs.

'One minute,' said Sylvia.

I stopped.

'You take so much trouble over people who are foreigners, total strangers. It is quite rare. You have given us presents. We did not give you anything.'

'That's perfectly all right.'

'Take this.' Inside a small beautiful box there were three hand-embroidered handkerchiefs. The initials 'SM' were monogrammed on all three. They had been custom-made for her personal use. Sylvia Morris. 'SM'.

'They are very beautiful. If I ever have a daughter who can use them, I'll name her Sylvia.'

'Thank you so much.'

'You may even meet her, perhaps.'

'If I stay on in your country.'

Professor Dubley died that evening. We inquired everywhere and searched high and low for Sylvia to give her the news. We could not find her.

6

It was twenty-two years since all those events had come to pass. Dalpathado was standing in front of me; he was clasping my shoulders as if to console me.

I straightened up. 'I can't tarry any more. I must leave immediately.'

'Let the rain stop. I'll make arrangements.'

'The rain won't stop. I am already drenched. If I can reach Meenambakkam station from here, then I'll have nothing to worry about.'

'But I'll have to worry.'

'About what?'

'Let's wait for another hour or two. I can't help worrying about those two who were in the car last night.'

'What do you fear?'

'I can't tell you. There is a lot that they can do. The fact that you know me well enough to call my name out loud could endanger your life.'

'So, what are you doing here that can put you in such grave danger?'

Dalpathado did not speak. I didn't think that he would give me an answer. I stroked my cheeks. I should have shaved yesterday. Since I hadn't, my cheeks were rough with stubble, mostly grey. If I went out and someone was moved by my pathetic appearance to give me alms, it wouldn't surprise me at all.

Dalpathado must have been as old as I was. No, he had to be at least five or six years older. He must have crossed fifty. He had lost a lot of hair, but he was not noticeably bald. His face was as smooth as the outer skin of a plantain stem. No one could call him a young man; at the same time, he didn't look old either.

'In fact, I couldn't remember you at first.'

'I didn't need to. I've seen you many times on the road.'

'That means you must be staying in this city.'

Dalpathado merely smiled.

'I thought of Sylvia first. I remembered your name only after that.'

'It's been many years since Sylvia went out of my life.'

'I saw it coming.'

'When?'

'When you had come to India as a film producer. Twenty-two years ago.'

'My life and world were simple and uncomplicated then.'

'Even the film you brought to the festival was very simple.'

'Do you remember that too?'

'*Paranimaaru*, was it?'

'Yes, yes. You have such a good memory.'

'Didn't they give you an award for that film?'

'The prize and the medal disappeared a long time ago. I don't think even a single print of the film has survived.'

I tried to imagine him once again as a young man, an idealist who had revered Professor Dubley as a hero, a man who had thrown away his personal life and family inheritance because he wanted to make world-class films, an innocent artiste—as Dalpathado. What I had seen of him on that distant day bore no resemblance to the man before me. What was he doing? Why should our paths cross again?

Sivanesan burst in excitedly. He waved a finger at Dalpathado and summoned him. Dalpathado leapt up and followed him out of the room. I got up and tried to open the window, but couldn't because the slats were nailed to the frame and it was boarded shut.

I went to the next room. There, Dalpathado and Sivanesan were pushing a heavy box across the floor. Without it being starkly visible, a wooden plank had been fixed on the floor under the box. Dalpathado lifted the plank and Sivanesan climbed into the pit below. Dalpathado handed a couple of boxes and a suitcase to him. After stowing them safely in that secret pit, Sivanesan climbed out.

Dalpathado turned around and saw me. Sivanesan too looked at me and cast a questioning glance at Dalpathado. Dalpathado signalled with his eyes to indicate that there was nothing to fear on my account.

That room, as well as the one I had slept in, hardly looked like they were part of a functioning household. There was dust on the floor, with cigarette butts and matchsticks tossed haphazardly along the walls. On a small wooden object was a stove and three or four small utensils. The tea must have been prepared there that morning.

Sivanesan peered out through a gap in one of the window slats. After staying rigid for some time, he let his body gradually be at ease again.

'Not here,' he informed Dalpathado.

'What's the matter?' I asked Dalpathado.

'Remember those two who tried to kill me last night?'

'Did they follow us actually intending to kill you?'

'Do you doubt it?'

'How would I know? You told me that they posed a danger to me. You told me that my recognizing you and calling out your name was a blunder. But I don't know how or why.'

'It is I who should be so angry, not you. Those two did not know that I was Dalpathado. They recognized me because of you.'

'But why should they try to kill you?'

'It could be an order from their leader.'

'Who is their leader?'

'What would be the point of telling you? He must be someone from our country. He was my classmate, in fact. I was a rich man then; he was an ordinary chap.'

'How does he know that you are here?'

'Many of us worked together as recently as a year ago. Here, in this city of Madras.'

'In this house?'

'No. This is a new house. They don't know about it yet. Actually, since last night we have been facing a major crisis because of you.'

'You've said this over and over again.'

'No. Like you told me a short while ago, I haven't been able to communicate anything fully yet. Doing so could lead to problems on many fronts: my security, keeping this place secret, your security, and the risk of this house being discovered by them because of you. Not only that, but the work of a lifetime, all our plans and preparations, might also be blown to bits.'

'All this is fine, but I want to know something immediately.'

'What?'

'I don't normally pace up and down in a four-by-four room for so long after sunrise. And I couldn't go home last night. I would like to know if I can go my own way right now.'

Even as I was saying this, I noticed Sivanesan signal to Dalpathado that I couldn't. But the faint measure of confidence I still had in Dalpathado remained intact.

Dalpathado looked at his wristwatch. 'It's a quarter to seven now. I'll tell you at seven sharp. It will take that long for my concerns to be resolved.'

I went looking for my clothes. They were not only wet, but also streaked with mud and slush. How was I going to explain all this to my wife?

I put on my clothes, and folded and put away the lungi that Dalpathado had given me the previous night. I didn't really need to treat it with such respect. If it was taken in for washing, it would take a lot of water to rinse it properly. Whose lungi was it? Who else came to that house apart from the three of us? Who else stayed there? This was like the waiting room in a railway station, except that there were many chairs in a waiting room. In that house, there were just a few mats, lungis and some cardboard cartons—that was all.

I heard Dalpathado and Sivanesan speaking to each other in a low murmur. Dalpathado spoke to me mostly in English. On a couple of occasions, he tried to speak to me with the little bit of Tamil he knew. Sivanesan was surely a man who was fluent in Tamil. But the language in which those two spoke to each other was neither Tamil nor English. Sivanesan spoke in a tone of rebuke and warning. Dalpathado spoke to him in an appeasing manner.

Suddenly I recalled something. Though these two looked Indian, they were in fact foreigners. They might have come to India because of the political chaos prevailing in their own country. Many more people from their country were living all over south India.

Even refugee camps had been set up to house them. Was it possible to consider Dalpathado a refugee? How was he able to go in and out of the airport with such ease? Was he a passenger yesterday, or a spectator, or a member of the airport staff? If he was a passenger, which flight had he been on? Did he arrive from Singapore or Bombay?

Along with these questions, the events I had witnessed earlier made me anxious. The speed at which the car had come at us last night was certainly homicidal; when it passed us once and came back looking for Dalpathado again, the same frenzy was evident. Fortunately, he had eluded their eye. He was smart enough to have got away. Perhaps these situations were not uncommon in his life? How did I get entangled in their problems?

I started to feel hungry. A benefit of reaching the age of fifty was that you didn't need a lot of food. But when you were hungry, you felt more helpless than an infant.

Dalpathado must have been hungry too. Sivanesan must have been as well. But they were acting as if they didn't know that a man had to eat to survive. Dalpathado was older than me but had a firm physique. His body had been nurtured for many long years on healthy, nutritious food. It was immediately apparent that Sivanesan came from an average family of average means. But he was younger than us by many years. I was the only one who was suffering from hunger, thirst and skipping my morning ablutions.

I tried to open the other window in the room. The rain had let up a little. Since all the windows were shut, only a small amount of light had spread in the room.

I couldn't open it. However, because the slats were made of cheap planks, gaps had appeared between them. The window faced due east. I tried to peer through a gap but could see nothing but barren land for miles. A couple of small houses in the distance. A row of tall coconut trees. My eyes could not see further. Beyond them must have been the sea. These areas were suitable for people who thought they had had enough of life and wanted to live in relative seclusion. As Madras city continued to expand, houses sprang up in areas that were once fallow and slushy. The suburban train service was crowded at all hours with people of all ages and classes. But no one had come to live in that rocky area. Even those who had made the mistake of building houses there could only expect the likes of Sivanesan and Dalpathado to rent them. What could we call them? Murderers? Robbers? Smugglers? Foreign terrorists? Amidst these thoughts, I was reminded of Dalpathado's wife. Even he had had to give up his wife and children in order to live with Sylvia. And he parted from Sylvia in Madras. Then he could have gone back to his wife and children, couldn't he? Wasn't that how it happened in the movies? But why had he come to this country and what was he doing here?

Dalpathado came into the room. 'Forgive us,' he said. 'You must stay with us the whole day today, until sunset.'

7

The world doesn't come to a halt because a tragedy has occurred. After one or two days, even those who have personally experienced that grief resume their daily lives.

After Lalitha got married and left home, initially nothing appeared to have changed. She visited us once a week along with her children. Occasionally, she would leave a child in our care, and I would go to her house to drop the child back. After marriage, her responsibilities increased in manifold ways. Functioning like a personal secretary to her husband, she had to pay attention to matters which were completely unrelated to the family: sort an enormous pile of documents into categories and file them away; prepare notes and check the details of accounts written down on large sheets of paper filled with lines.

She had to note down and supply the information that her husband and his company had to submit frequently on government forms, ensuring that there was no discrepancy from one instance to the next. She had to follow up regularly on the complaints and applications that her husband's company routinely filed in the courts and with various government departments. She had to fulfil more responsibilities than I could comprehend. Where and when she had learnt it all remained a puzzle to me. Could an ordinary graduate learn so many business techniques in such a short time and also use them so skilfully? After meeting the needs, commands and demands of everyone at home, including her father-in-law, mother-in-law, children and relatives, how was she able to participate so readily and intensely in the world of business, which had so many intricacies, rules and regulations? The major improvement in her husband's performance and its contributory factor were immediately obvious to his business partners. In fact, they wanted Lalitha to be directly involved in the affairs of the company. The overseas tour might have been a ruse to realize their intention. After all, during all those years spent in the corporate environment, they hadn't thought a whole lot about wives.

I didn't know any of this while Lalitha was still alive. Even after she grew into an adult, got married and gave birth to children, the image associated in my mind with the name 'Lalitha' bore no relation to her actual appearance and personality—I discovered this only after she was no more. After she passed away, whenever I tried to recall her, no distinct image surfaced in my mind. If someone had asked me, 'What did your daughter look like? Can you mention some of her features?' I would be stumped. I couldn't even recall her height and complexion. Was this why I had not travelled to Bombay, deciding that her husband would identify her body? When her corpse arrived in Madras, was this why I had not gone there even to get a glimpse of the box or attend her cremation?

But not even a month had passed before I went looking for her. I couldn't recall her physical form. I could say, 'This is Lalitha' if I saw her, but I couldn't cite the distinguishing marks which identified her as Lalitha to me. It had been several months since her physical markers had mingled with the earth, wind and sea. How could I see her and talk to her without any physical contact? I wanted to confess to her, 'I raised you into adulthood, but I never had a good look at you, not even once.' I wanted to plead with her, 'My darling daughter, I spent twenty-two years without knowing who you were. Now I can no longer see you or touch you. Will you please forgive me?'

Her old suitcase, pillow, geometry box, clothes and handkerchief were strewn all over our house but did not give me the hope that any of them would bring her back to me. There was a handkerchief on which the initials SM were embroidered beautifully. It was very old; in fact, Lalitha and the kerchief were of the same age. There was no connection between the letters SM and her name. But this handkerchief, along with two more, was given to her when she was three years old. She had preserved them as though they were some kind of treasure. Two of those kerchiefs had become frayed and tattered. This one alone had remained intact. A handkerchief had survived for twenty-two years. Instead of accompanying her to her in-laws' home, it had stayed behind with us.

That handkerchief did not remind me of Lalitha. Instead, it made me recall how another girl in a bewildered state had felt helpless one day. There stood a man in front of me who reminded me of that girl. Just as long-buried phantoms rise when wells and ponds are dredged, that ghost had risen after twenty-two years. What was the connection between me and that ghost? No connection, except that I had met, talked to and interacted with Dalpathado for a week. Sylvia at least had left behind a few handkerchiefs. This man, when he left, had evoked only pity and doubt in my heart.

I remembered Sylvia's name. I also remembered her face. In fact, I even remembered the perfume she had worn. Even after twenty-two years had rolled by, the picture of her from that day, sniffling while trying unsuccessfully to stifle her sobs, was fresh in my mind. To say it had stayed fresh was wrong, perhaps; something which lay buried somewhere had, as soon as I set eyes on Dalpathado's face, risen from the unfathomable depths to occupy my whole mind. But the reason I had gone to the airport was to bring back another face into my consciousness—the face of my daughter who had lived in front of my eyes for twenty-two years, but which I couldn't conjure up in the midst of my thoughts. It was there that I had last seen her alive. And it was there that I could have seen her half-charred corpse for the first and last time.

I had grown accustomed to electric trains. The constantly changing nature of electric trains from six in the morning to ten at night had become familiar to me in all its minute details. The Meenambakkam segment of GST Road stretched ahead for me to scour it inch by inch. The wind, clouds, stars and the rising moon kept soundlessly urging in my ears, 'Get to know me! Learn more!' I didn't know if I had been noticed by them, but I had paid enough attention to the people in the locality to be able to recognize most of them. Airport staff, vehicles that frequented the airport, arrival and departure timings of various flights, policemen, taxi and autorickshaw drivers, tea-stall owners, petty shopkeepers, anonymous strangers who kept loitering in the airport area for no apparent reason, those who came to pick up women, those who solicited on behalf of women, rowdies, pickpockets, buses which halted at the bus stop, buses which were slightly less crowded, bus conductors, winged white ants, moths, beetles that got into your hair and ears, snakes, frogs, bandicoots—all these things had caught my eye. I knew them well. But I still could not see my daughter Lalitha's face. If her destiny had been robust and she had lived, the flight on which she was to arrive in Madras from Bombay would have landed only after dusk. Instead of waiting for that flight, she boarded one that would depart from Bombay at an unearthly hour and land in Madras at an equally unearthly hour. Did she actually board that flight? Didn't she trip on her feet and stumble? Didn't it occur to her not to travel at an hour when ghosts roamed about? Didn't anyone tell her? She was in such a hurry and so excited to see her children again. Having waited for a whole month, she could have waited one more day. She didn't, and everything was lost. Even the fact that there was someone called Amma would have faded from her children's awareness. When even a fifty-year-old like me could not recall her face, how could her small children remember anything? Only the faces of grandmothers with grey hair and the criss-cross of wrinkles on their foreheads and cheeks, women who fed them milk from feeding bottles, would have stayed in their minds.

But I was unable to carry on like the children. I couldn't, like my wife did, wail and cry four times and then go off to do the next round of household chores. What an omnipotent boss these household chores were! A woman could cry—or laugh, or sleep, or relax—only if that boss permitted it. This master must have issued relentless commands to Lalitha too. Instead of waiting to receive orders, she would have fulfilled them on her own. There was no grief for those who always had tasks to perform. Even if they had things to grieve over, they could not amplify their sorrow and spend all their time mourning.

If I didn't have this grief, what would there be to live for? This, too, was a lie—what was not there? Lalitha was not there. Only Lalitha was no more. But when she had been alive, what big difference had it made? I had not spoken soothingly with her for half an hour, or petted her children, or asked her about her troubles and difficulties. I had been so without affection that I couldn't even retain the memory of her face in my mind. It was that sense of shortcoming that made me wander around the airport, insistent that I must see her again, even if she was a ghost or an apparition. Even if she hadn't openly asked me for anything, she too must have had lots of wishes and aspirations. Her death, which had occurred at a time when none of them were yet fulfilled, would make her seek out this earth over and over again. With her rare good nature, she would not subject her husband, children or mother to unearthly experiences. Therefore, she would not come anywhere near her home. Therefore, she must be hovering around in this Meenambakkam area. I would certainly see her. 'My darling! When you were alive, I didn't cosset you lovingly. I've come to you now!' I would scream. I could sense Lalitha's presence. Lalitha! Lalitha!

8

As soon as Dalpathado told me that I couldn't go home before sunset, I rolled up the lungi in my hand and flung it away. Since that gesture was unexpected, Dalpathado was startled.

'I am hungry. I must have a bath. First, I have to go to the toilet,' I said.

'Let the rain stop for a bit. I will arrange everything. The toilet is right here, outside the house. You might get wet.'

'It doesn't matter.'

Sivanesan signalled his disapproval to Dalpathado. Ignoring him, Dalpathado led me to the first room and opened the door. A spray of pelting rain burst into the room. He found a large carton, the kind pharmacies or grocery stores use to stack dozens of bottles of Horlicks or tonic, and covered my head with it. Draping something like a waterproof jacket over his own head, he led me outside. The rain was pouring steadily. Although I couldn't see beyond ten feet, I could sense that there was no other human in that area. Along the side of the house was a small room. Other than in the rainy season, the arrangement was unlikely to cause any difficulty. We needed to be cautious about one thing, though: in such places a snake often lay coiled up in a corner.

Dalpathado, too, was getting drenched in the rain as he stood guard over me. I was amused by the high opinion he had of my physical prowess and my sense of independence. Even if he had given me a shove and said, 'Go!' what could I have done? I would have again stood huddling by the wall of that house, seeking shelter from the rain. The railway station must have been at least two or three miles away. If someone didn't take me there, I was not at all confident of finding my own way. Even though Dalpathado was involved in clandestine activities, he still treated me like a friend.

Sivanesan made me another cup of tea. Then he put on a raincoat and stepped out. Dalpathado turned on a small radio. The news was being read out in Tamil.

Disturbed conditions in many parts of the world. The armed forces of a superpower had landed in another country. Hostages had been shot and flung on top of a rubbish heap. New projects for the development of the country's hill tribes. The government's special plan to provide drinking water to every village. A top tennis player had beaten another. A third player had vanquished a fourth. Over the next twenty hours, widespread rains were expected in Tamil Nadu. Madras and its environs would receive intermittent rains, with heavy showers on a few occasions.

Turning the dial of the radio, Dalpathado stopped at a station playing Hindi film songs. A thirty-year-old song came on air. We exchanged glances.

'If it's a Suraiya song, I'll drop whatever I am doing and sit down to listen. I will resume only after the song is over,' said Dalpathado.

'At one time, she was my favourite singer too. But there weren't so many female singers then, right?'

'Are there a lot of them now?'

I couldn't answer that question immediately. 'Not really. But it seems like there are many female singers now, and very few women used to sing in those days.'

'That's merely an illusion. We take many decisions believing that such illusions are true. There were indeed many female singers around thirty or forty years ago. Apart from them, some actresses sang their own songs. Thanks to them, we could listen to a variety of voices and singing styles.'

'Anything you say about film-related matters has to be right. But weren't you making films without songs even in those days?'

'Does that mean I don't like film songs? I love listening to Indian film songs, especially Hindi songs.'

'In those days, you couldn't listen to a song whenever you felt like it. But now, there are so many facilities: records, cassettes and tapes. I am sure you have them all.'

'I did, a long time ago. In those days, only a German tape recorder—Grundig—was available. It used to be chunky like a typewriter but its performance was superior to any of the later models. We used that tape recorder even for our film shoots.'

'When did you go back to your country?'

'When? I don't understand your question.'

'I meant the time you had come to India with Sylvia.'

The smile on Dalpathado's face was not one of cheer. 'Well, I couldn't afford to stay on here for long. What could I do? I couldn't bring money here. I couldn't earn even a paisa here. On the last three days of that trip, I didn't even have enough money to eat properly.'

'But you keep visiting India again and again.'

Dalpathado did not reply.

'What are you doing here?'

'Just a minute,' said Dalpathado. He went to the next room and fetched a pack of cigarettes from a bag kept in an alcove there. He sat in front of me and lit a cigarette. It was a foreign brand.

'What were you asking?' Dalpathado began.

'Are you making any films now? What are you doing in this country?'

Dalpathado laughed wryly this time. 'Who wanted my cinema, anyway? I had to give up so much to make *Paranimaaru*! I had to put up with so much humiliation just to be able to show it to a few people. What happened in the end?'

'You shouldn't be asking me any questions. I don't know much about all this.'

'Do you know who my ideal film-maker was in those days? Mr Satyajit Ray of your country. It was after seeing one of his films that I vowed that films of that quality would be made in our country too. And I did make such a film. Nobody in my country would touch it. It was then that your festival came along. I had to beg at the feet of all kinds of people before I managed to come to your country with a print of my film. You gave me a prize, gave me an award. You made me throw a party. What happened, finally? I had to scrounge in your airports, unable to afford even porter's charges for my bag and baggage. I could just as well have stayed home.'

'Why did you stop with just that one film? You could have tried to make a few more.'

'Who told you I stopped with one film? I made four after *Paranimaaru*. Three were left incomplete. For that one completed film, do you know who I had to borrow money from?'

'I don't know. Except your name, I don't know anything about you.'

'I went to my former wife and took a loan from her. She lent me some of the money she had extorted from me. I didn't return it.'

'Didn't she ask for it?'

'Of course she did. I took all the reels of my film and dumped them in her house. "This is one of the world's greatest art treasures; you can't measure its value with money," I told her. She fell about laughing.'

'I am very hungry.'

'You have to wait for some more time. Siva will come now. If those two men had not come chasing after you and me, we wouldn't have had these problems. You would have gone your own way. We would have stayed here.'

'Who are those two? Are they henchmen of your classmate?'

'Do you know them?'

'Would I ask you if I did?'

'I don't know for certain, either. But surely, those who come looking for me do not come to felicitate me, but to finish me off. Because you made it appear as if you knew me, they would have targeted you as well.'

'Are you keeping me here to protect me, or to finish me off yourself?'

'I regret not being able to tell you anything. I don't mean any harm to you. After this one day is over, everything will become clear.'

'What business do you have in this country, in this city?'

'Where do you think I should go, instead of here?'

'I don't know. Why are you here? What are you doing?'

'I can't answer all your queries and doubts. But there's one thing I can say—as soon as I set foot in my country, I'll be taken into custody.'

'By whom?'

'By the government in my country. The state police.'

'Why? What for?'

'I'll tell you this much. I've been declared an enemy, a traitor to our country. In most countries, traitors are put to death.'

'Why are you staying here, then?'

Dalpathado did not reply.

'It looks like neighbouring countries are obliged to offer refuge to traitors,' I said.

'At the same time, they also provide shelter to spies, it seems.'

'What are you saying?'

'Remember those two who came to kill me yesterday? I was referring to them.'

'Didn't you say you didn't know who they were?'

'It is only a guess.'

'What?'

'That they belong to our government's intelligence agency.'

'How is that possible? Can spies roam around so freely here?'

'Do you know there are hordes of spies in this country? The locals don't know, but we do.'

'When I see the range of things that a formerly idealistic film-maker has learnt and mastered in these twenty years, I am simply amazed.'

Dalpathado did not reply. I found the situation quite insane. How could a man like me, driven to insanity by the loss of a beloved daughter in an accident and also by other setbacks in life, mock another man who was striving towards a goal, even putting his own life at stake? I could, of course, be angry with Dalpathado for disrupting my daily routine and holding me in captivity. But I didn't feel much anger. The past ten or twelve hours had been spent in a manner that was completely incompatible with my way of life. I should be angry with Dalpathado for this, but in truth, I was not angry at all. My life had indeed become meaningless to me. Even lack of sleep was not a concern for me; only hunger still remained a sensation worthy of articulation. Once that hunger was assuaged, I would return to my inert state.

I felt an urge to ask Dalpathado about Sylvia. He spoke about everything under the sun, but he never uttered a word about her. It was Sylvia who had played the female lead in his award-winning film *Paranimaaru*. In that film, she played a village belle who had no trace of the urban spirit. A guileless face. A face that exuded optimism. A strong woman who did not flinch from hard work and the burden of life's sorrows. In fact, Sylvia too should have got the Best Actress award at that festival. She must have lost out by a slender margin.

Dalpathado kept smoking one cigarette after another. That small house was soon filled with tobacco smoke. After a point, I couldn't bear it. 'Open the door,' I said as I motioned with my hand. Dalpathado put out his cigarette and walked over to open the door. Just then, there was a knock on the door. It was a coded knock, in the same way that Dalpathado had knocked last night. He opened the door. Sivanesan stepped inside carrying a suitcase and a bag.

9

Sivanesan looked meaningfully at Dalpathado and said, 'All set.'

Dalpathado took the suitcase from him and kept it carefully next to the wall. 'Come, let's eat something,' he said to me and went into the next room. He filled two glasses with water and placed them on the floor. Sivanesan lit the stove again.

Dalpathado sat on the mat and took out a few packets from the bag Sivanesan had brought. 'Hello, masala dosa!' he said. Some of the packets were triangular in shape. Dalpathado opened the masala dosa packets and placed them before me. 'Please eat,' he said.

'Isn't Mr Sivanesan eating with us?'

'He ate first before buying food for us.'

'How do you know?'

Dalpathado shrugged his shoulders.

His appetite was astonishing. Till then, not even a small sign of exhaustion or fatigue had appeared on his face. Nor did I see any sign of his having slept little the previous night. But the way he started eating and demolishing packet after packet of food would have amazed anyone. My hunger was gone after I consumed two idlis. Sivanesan made tea for us again.

I wondered whether Dalpathado's bingeing was meant to compensate for his excitement about something. The relaxed air he had about him before Sivanesan's arrival was gone. He did not speak much or fuss about anything. But I could somehow sense that he was thinking about something with single-minded focus.

I was about to open the door to go out and wash my hands when Sivanesan leapt up at lightning speed and stopped me. He had kept two suitcases open in that room. He had been removing all the objects from the pit and keeping them next to the suitcase. I had to wash my hands with water in a corner of that room.

After devouring the food in all the packets, Dalpathado started smoking again. 'Close the door!' shouted Sivanesan. I went to the room where Dalpathado was sitting. He shut the room door.

'What do we do now?' I asked.

'I'll tell you. Please wait for some more time.'

'How long?'

'Until this evening. After that, even if you want, we are not going to keep you with us.'

Sivanesan knocked on the door.

'What is it?' Dalpathado asked him.

'Open the door,' replied Sivanesan, his tone a bit harsh.

Dalpathado opened the door. I went with him to the adjoining room. The suitcases were shut. Sivanesan gathered all the scraps of paper in the room along with a few packets and pushed them to a corner.

Then, he climbed down into the pit. Dalpathado picked up a suitcase and handed it to him to stow carefully inside. The pit was big enough to accommodate three or four suitcases. It couldn't even be called a cellar. They had dug a trench, that was all. Its sides were not paved with cement. Sivanesan and Dalpathado must have dug it together.

After putting both suitcases inside the pit, Sivanesan covered it with the plank. 'Get me the money and the papers,' he told Dalpathado.

Dalpathado raised his hand to the ventilator in that room. Only then did I spot the small leather bag that had been kept there. Dalpathado opened the bag, looked inside and said, 'Puss-port?' Most people from Dalpathado's country habitually shortened the long vowel.

'Look in your zip bag,' he told Sivanesan.

The rain had stopped completely. We could hear two children playing in the house next door.

When I had stepped out to go to the bathroom a short while earlier, I got the impression that there was no human presence in the three or four houses adjoining ours. Now it was clear that at least one family resided there.

Sivanesan went out again. Both he and Dalpathado seemed to be animated by a new fervour and excitement. Dalpathado gathered all the objects in the house, not too many, in the front room. There were very few clothes among them. With a brush and water, he started washing the clothes he had worn the previous night. The fabric was made of synthetic fibre. I was amazed by his skill and realized that he must have washed clothes in this fashion many times before.

Dalpathado cleaned Sivanesan's clothes carefully, the rest he folded and put away. I wanted to give him my clothes too. However, he next collected everything from every nook and corner of that house—bits of paper, empty cigarette packs and matchboxes, cardboard boxes, discarded leaves from food packets and plastic bags—and gathered them carefully in the centre of that room. It was a house roofed with Mangalore tiles. The entire area where the wall supported the roof was used as a loft. It was from there that Dalpathado retrieved many items. Along with soap, a shaving kit and comb, there were also pliers, spanners and screwdrivers in there. In addition, there was a roll of thin wire. Dalpathado stuffed all the paper scraps and cardboard boxes into a large plastic bag. The clothes he had cleaned were still drying. Laying a mat on the floor, he spread out the clothes on it in such a way that the damp portions were exposed to the air. His shoes looked special. He took both socks out of them, pulled them straight and laid them on the floor to dry. He scanned the walls thoroughly for letters and numbers, and erased them if he found any.

At first, I merely observed his activities. I understood that he was making arrangements to vacate that house. His actions were marked by professional skill. He must have been used to vacating houses in this fashion. Sleep was making my eyelids heavy. I thought briefly about my wife. Lalitha's husband had asked her to come to his house immediately. It was Lalitha's younger child's birthday. After a year of ritual mourning following Lalitha's death, this was the family's first celebration. My wife wouldn't even know that I had been away from home the whole night. Ants must have invaded the rice and buttermilk that she would have kept for me. I wondered what time she was planning to return home.

By then, Dalpathado had folded the lungis too. He retrieved two high-quality nylon bags from the loft and placed them on the floor. They were large bags, with caster wheels fitted to the base. He picked up the clothes that were arranged in separate piles and stacked them neatly in those bags.

'Will you spare me one of those mats? I feel like lying down,' I told him.

Dalpathado cleared a mat for me. I spread the mat in the room where I had spent the night, lay down on it and stretched my legs. I fell asleep immediately.

10

When I woke up, the house was brightly lit. It must have been three or four in the afternoon. There was no one at home. Both Dalpathado and Sivanesan had locked the house from outside and gone out somewhere. There was tea in a tumbler next to the kitchen stove. It must have been kept there for me.

Both the nylon bags were neatly packed and closed. There was not a piece of paper or rubbish in the house. I removed the plank covering the pit that they had dug in the front room and took a look inside. The two suitcases were still there. They were neither large nor very small. With a bit of effort, a man could walk carrying both. I replaced the plank as before and closed the pit. A clock seemed to tick away somewhere.

I didn't have to wait long. Dalpathado and Sivanesan returned soon. Along with excitement and determination, the relaxation that followed the completion of a task was also evident in their bearing. There was a cloth bundle in Dalpathado's hand.

Sivanesan did not speak to me. 'I had kept some tea for you. Did you drink it?' Dalpathado asked me in a friendly tone.

I didn't reply. 'We will say goodbye to each other only at seven o'clock this evening. After that, you may remember me if you want; or forget me. It would be better to forget.' I didn't speak.

'I would really like this one day's crisis to be over and done with today,' he added further.

'Tell him,' Sivanesan urged Dalpathado.

'Sure, I am going to,' replied Dalpathado. 'Go and bring the bicycle.' Sivanesan went out. Dalpathado latched the door.

'We will all be leaving in an hour. We are going out of the city. You can go home.'

'Are you planning to go back to your country?'

'To my country? Didn't I tell you that they would arrest me and hang me the moment I set foot there? We have to stay on in your country for some more time.'

'Your friend Sivanesan . . . is he going to be hanged too?'

'Yes. But there's something special in this situation. In our country, we might go hammer and tongs at each other, but here, we are both traitors to our nation.'

'May I leave?'

'No. We're all going to leave together, at least up to GST Road. After that, we need a little help from you.'

'What?'

'Take off your shirt. I'll give you a fresh one. Please put it on.'

Dalpathado opened the cloth packet he had brought. Inside it was a new shirt.

I removed my filthy shirt and put on the new one.

'Does it fit well?' he asked.

'Yes.'

A stove, two vessels, bottles, four glass tumblers, four spoons—Dalpathado fitted all of them together and took them in both hands. He also wedged the mat I had slept on under an arm. 'Could you please open the door? I'll give these to our neighbour and come back.'

I unlatched the front door and Dalpathado stepped out carrying the vessels and bottles. I stood at the doorstep and looked out. He walked to the farthest of the three small houses there, handed over everything and came back immediately.

'We'll leave as soon as Sivanesan comes back. Come, we'll wait inside.'

'But there is nothing for us to sit on.'

'Sit on a bag.' I sat on a nylon bag. There was a knock on the door. Sivanesan was back, bringing a rented bicycle with him.

Dalpathado retrieved the two suitcases from the pit in the front room. He looked pointedly at Sivanesan, who nodded.

Sivanesan mounted both suitcases on the luggage carrier of the bicycle. Taking a long nylon rope from his trouser pocket, he tied them securely to the bicycle. Dalpathado hung a nylon bag each on either side of its handlebars.

I started out, taking my dirty shirt with me. Dalpathado put it in a paper bag, turning it into a compact package.

As Sivanesan walked ahead, pushing the bicycle, Dalpathado trailed behind him, holding the suitcases in place. The rain had stopped and the ground had dried to some extent.

The evening traffic on GST Road was as busy as ever. Dalpathado removed both the nylon bags from the bicycle. He gave me a bag and said, 'Please carry this for some time.'

I slung the bag over my shoulder. Sivanesan had walked briskly ahead, pushing the bicycle with the suitcases. It seemed that Dalpathado was deliberately dragging his feet. When we were about ten feet away from the main entrance of the airport, Sivanesan came to us, carrying both suitcases. The bicycle was missing. The three of us stopped by the roadside for a minute.

'Now you have to do one more favour for us,' said Dalpathado.

'What is it?'

'This Sivanesan is a vicious man. He won't hesitate to kill anyone.'

'Is that so?'

'But you have to take the two suitcases from him and go to the airport.'

I couldn't understand what he was saying.

'It's nothing big. Sivanesan is a killer all right. You must take these suitcases and go immediately to the service counter of our national airline.'

'No. I won't.'

'Please don't say that. This is all you have to do. Here is Sivanesan's coat. Put it on. Take both suitcases and go to our airline counter. You'll find the ticket in the right pocket. There's a hundred-rupee note too. If you give them the ticket, they will tear off a foil and give you a boarding pass. Collect the pass and come out.'

'I think you are crazy.'

Sivanesan drew close to me. Dalpathado stretched out his hand and restrained him, saying, 'Stop.'

He said, 'If you don't want to, I won't compel you. We need to catch a train at Egmore around the same time.'

'Aren't you taking these suitcases with you?'

'No. Someone will collect them. All you have to do is hand over these two suitcases to our national airline and collect the boarding pass. That'll do.'

His ingratiating words and manner were like a dose of chloroform to me. I draped Sivanesan's coat on my shoulders and picked up the two suitcases.

I must have taken four steps when Dalpathado called out, 'If they ask for the passport, it is in the left pocket.'

I carried the suitcases and walked to the entrance. Automatic sliding doors were not in vogue then. I pushed the door open and entered the building. When we had come here to send off Lalitha, it was I who had held the door open.

The national airline of Dalpathado's country had its counter in a corner. An employee of the company was standing outside.

He placed the two suitcases on a weighing scale. It showed 33 kg. I took the plane ticket and the hundred-rupee note from the right pocket of Sivanesan's coat, and gave them to the attendant. He wrote '22 kg (two pieces)' on the ticket, tore off a foil and gave me the rest of the ticket along with a receipt for the baggage. He then pushed the two suitcases inside.

I didn't want to come out of the airport. I had a look at the ticket. It was bought for someone called Manuel. I took the passport out of the left pocket of Sivanesan's coat and looked at it. It had been issued by the government of his country. In the photograph, Manuel had a scowl on his face. If you didn't look at it closely, you might have thought that it was my photograph.

Outside, Sivanesan was waiting for me. I handed the coat to him. He crumpled the plane ticket and boarding pass, and shoved them into his pocket. He slipped the passport into his shirt pocket. 'Where is Dalpathado?' I asked him.

'He left. He told me to give your shirt back to you,' he said, and gave me the packet. 'I am going to Egmore by electric train. If you are coming with me, I'll buy a ticket for you too.'

'Those two suitcases?'

'They will reach our country on our airline's flight.'

'Won't they ask for the owner?'

'They may. Or they may not. So, are you coming to catch the train?' Sivanesan must have thought of something; he took out the crumpled airline ticket from his pocket, tore it

117

up and threw the bits away. 'So, are you coming?'
he asked me.

'No. I don't have to go anywhere in a
hurry.'

Sivanesan left immediately. Standing by
the roadside, I watched night descend on
Meenambakkam airport. My legs dragged me
involuntarily towards the terminal building.
I couldn't go inside without a ticket. As usual,
I peered through the plate-glass window. The
domestic flights section was crowded. Two
flights were to leave shortly.

I moved on and looked at the overseas
section through the glass. Around the counter
of the national airline of Dalpathado's country,
there was a lot of bustle. It was nearly time for
the flight to depart.

I stood watching the passengers. Anyone
would wonder why a grown man was peering
in from outside, like a child watching an
unfamiliar sight, with his face pressed against
the glass. My eyes travelled suddenly to that

corner. There, the two suitcases given to me by Sivanesan were kept along the wall. They had not been loaded on the flight. Serves that rogue right, I thought.

I went home. My wife had not returned yet from Lalitha's husband's house.

I threw out the stale rice and put the vessel away for washing. I made tea and drank a cup. It was tea prepared with milk powder. Sivanesan too must have used milk powder to make the tea. What could he have packed in those suitcases? Surely a table clock. It was the clock that was ticking constantly. It could have been an alarm clock too. If he had set the alarm for a particular hour, the clock would start ringing loudly when it was time. I stood up abruptly. It was indeed an alarm clock. But when the set hour was reached, it wouldn't start ringing; it would explode. The explosion would demolish the building and kill a lot of people. This was apparently what Dalpathado meant when he said treason. It must have been set to explode when the flight reached the airport terminal in their country. That was why neither he nor anyone else who knew about the suitcase had boarded the flight. Those suitcases were lying in a corner of the overseas travellers' section of Madras airport. They were going to explode at the appointed hour.

I was shocked. The time was two minutes to nine.

I came out of the house. Should I go to the police? By the time they understood what I was saying, satisfied themselves that I was not a lunatic, and started taking action, it would have been too late. In that case, whom should I inform; how could I let them know?

I felt something in my pocket. I was wearing the shirt given to me by Dalpathado. He had kept a five-rupee note in it.

I went to the neighbourhood pharmacy and told the owner, 'I need to make a phone call.'

'Do you have a one-rupee coin?'

'Yes,' I lied. 'Do you have the telephone directory?'

120

His initial response was no, but his colleague picked up a tattered copy of the directory lying in a corner and gave it to me.

In my confusion, I searched everywhere in the directory. The airport number was not listed under 'airport'; it was in the section for central government departments.

I dialled that number. As soon as I heard a 'hello' from the other end, I yelled urgently, 'Hello! There are two suitcases in your international departure hall . . .'

'Sorry, please call the airline.'

The man had hung up. I dialled the number again. 'Hello, I am the one who called just a few seconds ago. I have serious suspicions about those two suitcases.'

'Try calling security, sir. The number is 432007.'

'Sir! Sir! Please don't disconnect. There isn't much time left. It has already been two hours since those suitcases arrived at the airport. Anything can happen at any moment.'

Ashokamitran

'What do you think will happen? What's in those suitcases?'

Even as he was speaking, there was a loud noise at the other end of the line, like the onset of an earthquake.

It was indeed like an earthquake that a bomb had exploded in the airport.

122

11

Officially, thirty-three bodies were recovered and their identities established. Hands, feet and heads that had scattered in all directions were matched and assembled. Even then, hands for three of the bodies were missing. Officials were forced to conclude that after being flung very far from the airport by the explosion, those limbs might have been carried off by some animals. Among the scattered heads, one bore no mark on the face but had a wound at the back of the head. On another head, it was impossible to discern the face. It was inferred from the back of the head that it had belonged to a girl.

Of the dead, nearly half were women. It was a flight to the Gulf. The women had begun their journey, along with their husbands, from many different locations. They had travelled up to Madras by train or bus. From Madras, they had to take a plane which was completely unfamiliar to them. After reaching the airport several hours before departure time, they were waiting in the international passengers section. Many were asleep on the floor. They didn't know that they were going to die; not only that, they didn't even know that they had died. A second after the bomb exploded, they had turned into lifeless corpses, with their hands, feet and heads strewn everywhere.

One section of the airport was left without a roof. Its walls, air conditioning, electrical wiring and telephones had all been damaged and bent out of shape. There was blood everywhere. In the unlikeliest nooks and corners, there were bits of human flesh. Jewellery, personal belongings, chappals, shoes and caps. Someone's snuff box had hit the roof and dropped in the open area outside the airport.

I got there shortly after dawn. But there was a security cordon around the airport. All flights had been cancelled.

No one doubted that the explosion had been caused by those two suitcases. They had been taken right up to the aircraft, but because no one had claimed ownership, they had been brought back to the airport terminal and kept there. At that time, the idea that they might explode had not even occurred to anyone. Some passenger must have come all the way to the airport and then left in a hurry owing to some emergency, forfeiting his airfare and abandoning his luggage. What had happened to Mr Manuel? 'Mr Manuel, the aircraft is waiting for you. This is the last call for boarding. Please come immediately and board the flight. Mr Manuel! This is the last and final call!'

To whom could I confess that it was I who had brought those two suitcases to the airport and left them there? No one there was able to identify me. The person who had taken the suitcases from me had died in the explosion. There was no use looking for Manuel. They could only identify the person who had bought the ticket on behalf of Manuel.

Soon several other things came to light. At the time the flight was scheduled to land in the capital of the neighbouring country with those suitcases on board, jumbo jets belonging to two other foreign airlines would also have landed in that airport. Five hundred passengers in each of those flights. That suitcase bomb could have meant certain death for at least a thousand people. In Madras airport, it had taken between thirty-five and ninety lives.

A few more facts surfaced as well. Someone else who knew that the two suitcases had not been loaded on the flight was calling the airport officials for half an hour, even before me. Who was he?

I was in a state of total confusion. If I said anything to a stranger, he was not going to believe it. Two men had held me captive. These were their names. They were the ones who converted these suitcases into bombs. If I confessed that I was the one who carried those two suitcases into the airport on their behalf, it would be dismissed as the delusional rant of a lunatic bent on seeing his photograph in the papers. I only had insane-sounding replies to the questions that might be asked by the authorities.

Why did you come to the airport?

My feet pulled me in that direction without my knowing it.

Are you a lunatic that you visit places without being aware of it?

Not a lunatic. But no, I can't say that either. I could be insane.

Now, are you a lunatic or not?

No. I am the one who planted those bombs in the airport.

What kind of bombs, then?

I don't know what kind of bombs.

But you were the one who planted those bombs.

Yes.

I had an urge to go and look at the house where Dalpathado and Sivanesan had stayed. I was simply unable to find it. I roamed round and round those hillocks and that rocky area, but couldn't locate the house. I must have missed an important landmark. I just could not spot those tile-roofed houses.

By then it was confirmed knowledge—long before I made my call, someone had telephoned the airport, warning them of the danger from those suitcases. The airport officials must have been debating whether to believe his warning or not. Before they could finally decide that yes, it could be true, and act on it, the bomb had exploded.

Dalpathado! Dalpathado! Where are you?

I went again and again to the area near the airport. They had cordoned off the section of the airport where the bomb had exploded, and ensured that it remained out of bounds for everyone. Taking all kinds of emergency measures, they had facilitated the resumption of flights to and from the airport.

Security arrangements were beefed up in all Indian airports. People who came to receive or send off passengers were stopped outside the terminal building. Entry into the airport was strictly prohibited. All airport employees had to wear a photo identity card on their person, readily visible to anyone. Following the explosion, a few airport employees were even arrested on suspicion. Nevertheless, I kept wandering up and down GST Road.

I couldn't recognize the area during the day. Thinking that I would try after dark, I walked along GST Road one night. I looked for the spot where the car had tried to knock down

Dalpathado. At one point, the road took a slight turn. From there, I could see that construction work was under way at the site of the new airport terminal. I stopped at that spot, climbed down from the road and walked towards the rail tracks. When I reached the tracks, it was the hour when several express trains going south from Madras's Egmore station were scheduled to pass, one after another. I sat down on the narrow strip beside the blue metal stones of the track. The spot was adjacent to the track used by suburban trains. Once every five minutes, wheels bearing suburban train compartments rolled past me, almost within arm's reach. Light pouring out of the windows of those compartments was chopped into intermittent shafts, as from a film projector, and streamed past me. Because I was sitting so close to the rail track, light from the trains passing on it did not fall on me. Light from those passing on the next two tracks, however, did. Many passengers on those trains and their drivers could have seen me. To them it must have looked like I was sitting there only to watch those trains up close. I sat completely still, watching the trains that shook the ground as they thundered past me. I felt as though all my memories had faded away somewhere, and my entire existence was focused only on waiting for one train and then the next. In truth, this waiting had no worldly benefit. Therefore, it couldn't have offered any gratification to any of my senses. Waiting for a train, blending with it, waiting for the next one . . . During those moments, I forgot everything: myself, my wife, Lalitha, Dalpathado, Sivanesan, the large number of innocents who had died because of those two suitcases. Just me, those rail tracks and the trains. Every time a train rolled by, it felt like I was turning into that rail track, those wheels, those train compartments and those passengers. Not only that train and rail track, it felt like I was also turning into those blue metal stones. At the same time, it felt like I was turning into the ground as well. The ground travelled as far as the horizon and joined the sea and the sky. I had also turned into the sea and the sky.

Abruptly I changed back into a human who existed and functioned solely within his own body. I didn't know if what I had just experienced came about because of my grief or my sense of guilt. I felt that neither could be the reason. When a fifty-year-old man watching trains go by in the dark became one with his surroundings and the earth, how could it be from selfishness or egotism?

I stood up and crossed the tracks one after another. I recalled that when Dalpathado and I had crossed the tracks that night, we had taken a slight turn to the right. I turned a little to the right and walked on. Even in the dark, I knew that I was walking on rocks, not on ordinary ground. We had not walked on rocks that day.

It was a hillock that was half broken, one that had been chipped away gradually. After they started constructing houses using a mixture of cement and blue metal stone, the terminal period for granite mounds, particularly those that were situated near our big cities, had commenced. It must have taken forty or fifty years for this hillock to be hacked to half its size. There was a good chance that in the next thirty or forty years, there would be no trace of it left.

I retraced my steps in the dark. The clouds were galloping somewhere in a hurry. As a little boy, I was frightened by clouds moving across the night sky. When I was told that they looked small from the ground but were in fact gargantuan in size, I was able to imagine that perfectly. Because I perceived clouds to be bigger than the hillocks and mountains I had known, a cloud moving in the sky had always frightened me. On that day, although these clouds were unearthly in shape and size, I didn't find them fearful. Instead, I was overcome by grief.

I wandered around on that rough, uneven terrain for half an hour before returning to GST Road. Construction work for the second airport terminal was going on briskly. If I looked a little more intently, I could even see the workers in the distance engaged in their tasks. Work going on round the clock was meant to facilitate the handling of many more planes. More planes meant more passengers; more passengers meant the risk of many more people dying. Meenambakkam was already congested with the traffic of ghosts and the situation could only get worse.

As I kept walking along GST Road, I stopped in front of Meenambakkam airport. A flight from Bombay had arrived just then. It was on a similar flight that the remains of my daughter, whom I had scarcely known, had arrived like a parcel in a box. How had her husband recognized her? Among those dozens of charred corpses lying there, how had he identified someone as Lalitha? By the ornaments which were still stuck to the body? I didn't know what ornaments she was wearing. I never paid attention to her toe rings and things like that. I never saw my daughter Lalitha properly.

'You bastards! I was the one who planted that bomb!' I screamed twice. What I had screamed was incomprehensible even to me. Exhausted, I walked over to the terminal building. Apart from the fact that a portion of the building had collapsed, it did not appear to have been affected in any other way. In that damaged section, blood had spattered and dried in many spots on the ceiling. Along with blood, pieces of flesh too would have scattered. If the walls had not been cleaned properly, those pieces of flesh would have decomposed, emanating a stench. Airport authorities would have tolerated all kinds of hardships, waiting patiently for a return to normality, but they would not have tolerated the stench. The human body, even when it is alive, emanates a kind of odour. When the body is no longer alive, it gives off a different kind of odour. It's only these stinking bags of skin that we cherish as husband, wife, son, daughter, friend, enemy and so on.

That night too, I returned home at an unearthly hour when people were fast asleep and ghosts were frolicking about. After opening the door for me, my wife lay down on her bed again. In the kitchen, there was rice kept for me in a small vessel. On the shelf, there was a small quantity of buttermilk in a tumbler. After consuming both, I washed and stacked the utensils. I spread out my bedding and lay down. My wife was asleep by then. Her face grazed my hand. She must have been crying. The tears on her cheeks hadn't dried yet.

12

Only when I woke up the next morning did I learn about the envelope that had arrived for me the previous day. It must have been very elegant at the time it was posted. It was a beautifully designed pink envelope. The address on it had been struck off and corrected three or four times by different people. The letter had first reached the office where I used to work twenty years ago. It had travelled from there to another location, then another, and then, finally, to the place where I lived. I was amazed. The letter could have been returned to the sender from any of those locations with the stamp that says 'Addressee not found', but that had not happened. At each place, someone who was keen on the letter reaching me had written down my address as they knew it and posted it again. Since it had passed through many hands over many days, the envelope was filthy and ragged. I held it in my hands for some time without opening it.

My wife brought me a cup of tea. After twenty-three years of marriage, in certain moments we experienced a state where we didn't have to speak to each other at all. From where I was sitting I was able to sense, to some extent, her state of mind and mental conflict. Without even looking at me, she too could grasp what I was brooding over or feeling upset about. Not long ago, this became possible even when she and I were in different locations. But after Lalitha's untimely demise, either of us could divine the exact mental state of the other instantly. We did not worry about each other in the conventional sense. Anxiety arose only out of being in the dark about the other person.

My wife must have received the letter. She was not even curious about what it said or who had sent it. That it was from a world not familiar to her was not the reason for her indifference. The actual reason was that she didn't need to know. Our needs, even those related to knowledge, dwindled after a certain stage.

I gently tore open the envelope at one end. Even if I had crumpled and thrown it away without reading the letter, my act wouldn't have surprised or saddened me. I took the letter out of the envelope. It was lightly scented. When my olfactory sense had readied itself for the stench of decomposed human flesh, it must have become sensitive to every kind of smell. Normally, I wouldn't have known that the letter was scented. That day, it seemed as though I could even see the hand that had written it.

That hand, too, was a familiar one. Like a hand from some previous birth, I thought. The letter was from Sylvia. She had posted it to the address she knew as mine. Her letter, written two months earlier, had reached me only that morning.

Friend,

You are aware that an uncle of mine was living in a town called Bitragunta. During my visit to Madras twenty-two years ago, you had not only gone to the railway station to make inquiries but had also bought my train ticket to Bitragunta. My uncle passed away last year. He has nominated me to receive his provident fund amount after his death. I didn't know about it until now. My aunt left my uncle many years ago. When she lived with my uncle, a daughter was born to them. Her name was also Sylvia. She died when she was five. My uncle said often that my aunt was responsible for the child's death.

Be that as it may, I am coming to India again, courtesy of my uncle. I am eager to meet you next month.

140

*You will be reminded of something else
when you see this letter: Dalpathado. It has
been a long time since he left my life and our
country. You may be surprised to know that he
is considered a terrorist these days. If he is able
to persevere at something, he will be successful
at it. But he is destined to abandon everything
halfway.*

*This time, I am going to stay at a relative's
house in Royapuram. I have given the address
below. I will be staying in Madras for four days,
from the twenty-third to the twenty-sixth of this
month. I am very eager to meet you again. I will
call on you myself. If you can, try and visit me
in Royapuram.*

Sylvia

Not wanting to believe what I already knew,
I looked at the calendar. The date could not
be different for my sake—it was the twenty-
sixth. There had been no sign of Sylvia's arrival
in Madras. To track me down through all my

changes of address would have required plenty of time, which she might not have had.

Royapuram, too, was a locality where large numbers of people had lived and died. It was an area filled with iron, coal, ash and smoke. For nearly three hundred years, people of many countries and races—English, French, Portuguese, Armenian and Chinese—had walked on this soil, eaten and slept there. Many were also buried there. If Royapuram was one of the many localities in Madras that were inhabited by ghosts, Lalitha could well be hovering there, couldn't she?

I peeped inside the kitchen. After cooking a simple meal, my wife sat leaning against the wall, staring at the sky outside the door. Had she found out about my obsessive pursuit of ghosts? I had not seen a ghost yet, but had begun to feel that the day was not far.

I got ready to go out.

'Won't you be eating at home?' she asked.

'I'll come back in a couple of hours. You go ahead and eat.'

I travelled to Royapuram and searched for the address given by Sylvia. It was a locality where most of the residents were Indian Christians or Anglo-Indians. The fact that English was the language of people who were trapped in such dire poverty seemed to mock the prevalent Indian notion about English-speaking people. If English was the language of *durai*s,[4] these Anglo-Indians were born expressly to wring the conscience of that class of durais. Although their homes, dress, household articles and curtains across the front entrance were slightly different from the usual, none of that could hide the abysmal poverty in which they lived.

The address given by Sylvia was on a street where glamour and indigence were closely intertwined. On inquiry, I found out that an elderly woman lived in that dark cavern of a house with her grandson. When I reached there, only the grandson was at home, smoking a cigarette. He didn't bother at all about me.

'Has Sylvia Morris arrived or not? Tell me, da!' I asked in a loud voice.

'Who knows?'

'Why, don't you live in this house?'

'So what?'

'And you say you don't know?'

'Do I stay home all the time? Ask Grandma.'

I waited for his grandmother. She arrived carrying four or five packages in her hands. At first I couldn't understand what she was saying. Moreover, she spoke very fast. I often had to respond with brief questions.

There had been some change in Sylvia's itinerary. She hadn't arrived yet.

'If her flight comes at ten or twelve at night, what can I do? A trip to the airport costs a minimum of five rupees. I don't have any males here to assist me. What can I do?'

'Why is Sylvia coming here? Has she stayed here earlier?'

'She had come once, many years ago. My daughter was alive then. Sylvia is my aunt's daughter. She is going to inherit some property here. I'll get some money too.'

'Would you let me know when she arrives? I have known her for many years. She doesn't know my current address. I'll leave it with you. Please inform me immediately. You could even drop a postcard.'

'I am also waiting for her. We can barely afford our daily food. To cook for her when she is here, I bought a few items from the provision store.'

For some reason, I felt that the lady might have to wait forever. That grandson must be her daughter's child. What happened to his mother? I thought about the ways in which he must be harassing his old grandmother. He might not even know that if he subjected an old woman to such agony, her life would be cut short and that might affect him adversely. But miracles happened even in such situations. His grandmother's demise might show him a new path; give him a new lease of life. Those who were used to poverty could only spread more and more of it. The old woman's death might eliminate the character and signs of poverty from that house. Sylvia's uncle who had left her some money might have also suffered in poverty like them, but his money was going to help a young woman explore her special interests.

From Royapuram I walked via North Beach Road. I could catch the suburban train at Beach station and reach home punctually at the hour I had indicated to my wife. I was also somewhat hungry. At least today, I could avoid eating at an odd hour.

The moment I saw the train, my mind went berserk. Right there at that railway station, I began to feel as though I was transcending the limits of my body and wandering everywhere. I consciously arrested this feeling and boarded the train. I wondered whether Dalpathado could be travelling in that compartment. He was certainly in India, but he had to live in hiding and bide his time. By then, it was public knowledge that those who planted the bomb in the airport were from his country. From the press release issued by the High Commission, I learnt even the name of the political party that had planted the bomb. I, too, would be caught someday. Through me, they had a chance of finding out about the house where Dalpathado had stayed. But what clues could anyone find there? Sivanesan and Dalpathado were experts in their field. They took a long time to plan anything. When they executed it, they made it seem like a random event. If they hadn't found me that night, they would have found someone else. Suitcases carrying bombs would have reached the airport somehow. Perhaps they might even have reached the capital of their country and exploded there.

When Sylvia found out about my chance meeting with Dalpathado, how would she feel? At the time of her first visit to Madras, Dalpathado was her whole life. He was a film-maker with a sense of idealism. She was the main source of encouragement and cheer for him. She was an important factor behind his winning an international award. Without her cooperation and effort, his film *Paranimaaru* wouldn't have been possible. What would she say if she found out about Dalpathado's present circumstances? 'Poor boy, Dalpathado' is what she would say.

I found these circumstances extraordinary. Dalpathado must have been staying in Madras for a long time. But he stumbled into my view only two days ago. I got to spend nearly a whole day with him. Then I came home and found Sylvia's letter. This was a chance for me to meet them, a couple who had parted from each other more than twenty years ago; and a chance for them, through me, to meet each other!

Why hadn't Sylvia arrived yet? According to her letter, this was the day of her departure from Madras. If Sylvia's journey was delayed, couldn't she at least write a letter to that elderly lady, or send her a telegram?

This was how some people remained insensitive to other people's suffering. They had little or no concern for others. They had to achieve their goal, even if they had to put other people's lives at stake—like Dalpathado.

The columns upon columns of news reports about the bomb explosion in the airport stopped in just three days. The newspapers now awaited the next massacre.

The day after I made my trip to Royapuram, a four-line news snippet in connection with the airport mishap was published. A corpse that was grossly disfigured had been identified as the thirty-fourth fatality in the explosion. The name of the woman, who seemed about forty-five, was Sylvia Morris.

Notes

1   Manuneedhi Chozhan is a king of popular legend who is said to have dispensed justice in his kingdom with exemplary fairness. When his son, the royal prince, ran his chariot over a calf, its mother appealed to the king for justice by ringing the bell at the gates of the royal palace. The king ordered that his own son be punished by being crushed similarly under the wheels of a chariot.

2   A popular snack made of vegetable slices dipped in chickpea batter and deep-fried in cooking oil.

3   Half-sari, worn with a skirt by girls from puberty to late teens.

4   Term of address for colonial masters/overlords.

Notes

ALSO BY THE SAME AUTHOR

Still Bleeding from the Wound

Translated by N. Kalyan Raman

'Quirky and innovative in a way that only a
handful of our English-language writers, such
as Raja Rao and Vilas Sarang, have been'
Aravind Adiga

A perfect amalgam of irony, wit and wry humour,
Still Bleeding from the Wound is a collection of
stories from the greatest living Tamil writer.
Ashokamitran's deceptively simple narratives take
the reader deep into the poignant struggles waged
by ordinary middle-class men and women for
survival, dignity, and a hint of moral grace. His
nuanced prose is richly diverse in the range of
characters and situations they portray, marking him
as a master storyteller of our times.

Penguin Modern Classics/PB

Manasarovar

Translated by N. Kalyan Raman

**A profound meditation on the human quest
for faith and inner peace**

It is the early 1960s, also known as the golden age of
Indian cinema. Satyan Kumar, reigning screen god,
moves from Mumbai to the Madras film industry.
There he meets Gopalan, a middling studio writer.
An inexplicable connection forms between the two
men across the chasms of class and language. But just
as an enduring bond springs up, tragedy intervenes.

In spare unburnished prose, Ashokamitran
examines the finite human capacity to deal with pain
and sorrow and the need for redemption if life is to
go on. Brilliantly translated from the Tamil original
by N. Kalyan Raman, *Manasarovar* establishes
Ashokamitran as one of the most outstanding writers
of contemporary Tamil literature.

Penguin Books/PB

Fourteen Years with Boss

'It captures the reader from page one and the book keeps one absorbed from start to finish'—*The Hindu*

Reminiscing of a time long lost, *Fourteen Years with Boss* gives a delightful insight into the workings of Gemini Studios of Madras—one of the most influential film producing organizations in India—and its founder, the brilliant and multi-faceted S.S. Vasan.

Filled with vivid sketches of actors, extras, directors and the 'boss', Ashokamitran recreates life at the studio so that it materializes in the reader's mind with the perfect balance of humour and nostalgia.

Penguin Modern Classics/PB